curvy girl for the billionaire

emma bray

one

. . .

Charlie

I **SLIP** through the throng of midday pedestrians. The pulse of the city synchronizes with the throb of a headache I'm nursing.

It's another day where every penny clings to each other for dear life in my bank account. Charlotte "Charlie" Greene is my name, though the second part feels like a cruel joke. Green usually means go, or growth, or cash—things that seem just out of reach at the moment.

I started my event planning business the day I turned eighteen. A generous relative left me a sizable sum of cash, but it wasn't enough to live on for the rest of my life, so I thought I would do the smart thing and invest in a business doing something I loved.

It, coupled with a meticulous business plan, was enough to convince the bank that I meant business and secure the rest of the capital I needed to get my dream underway.

Three years later and my business is growing, but so are my bills. And rent here in the city isn't cheap. I just need a few more really good gigs and then I'll be out of debt and it'll all be profit.

Until then, the struggle is real.

My phone buzzes against the soft flesh of my hip, buried deep within the confines of my purse.

Shit, what now?

Fuck it, I'll check it later.

There are schedules to triple-check, venues to scout, and dreams to chase—even if they're wearing me thin.

The coffee shop on the corner is my first stop. It's not a luxury, but a necessity. The barista, a boy barely out of his teens, knows my order by heart. His eyes linger on the curves that my pencil skirt hugs unapologetically, but it's a look I've learned to ignore. I need caffeine, not a flirtation.

"Large Americano, extra shot," he recites, like a prayer offered to the goddess of overwork.

"Keep the change," I say, leaving a couple of dollars on the counter—my attempt at generosity, even when it hurts. I pivot on a heel, the air around me clinging to my body, heavy with the scent of freshly ground coffee beans and frothed milk.

Back on the street, I pass storefronts with mannequins dressed in clothes too expensive for their stillness, and restaurants where laughter spills out like music. None of it's for me. I have a mission: make this event planning business thrive, make Charlie Greene a name that echoes in the halls of high society, make it so my curves are synonymous with success and not struggle.

"Charlotte" might be etched on my birth certificate, but "Charlie" is the moniker that carries weight—the persona of a woman who doesn't flinch at challenge, whose ambition is as wide as her hips, and whose practical mind maps out her next move before the current one is complete.

My phone vibrates against the fabric of my pocket again. I sigh as I slip it out, fingers grazing the cracked screen—another expense on the never-ending list. The number is unfamiliar, but in this business, that's the harbinger of opportunity.

"Charlotte Greene," I answer, voice steady, exuding the confidence I meticulously craft.

"Ms. Greene, this is Claudia, assistant to Alexander Bennett."

The name hits like a shot of espresso straight to the veins. Alex Bennett.

The Alex Bennet.

Billionaire CEO, with eyes that command and a reputation that precedes him like a shadow on a sunny day. His world is one I've always viewed from the outside, pressed against the glass like a child at a candy store.

"Claudia," I respond with a practiced calm, even as my pulse begins to race. "What can I do for Mr. Bennett?"

"Mr. Bennett requires your expertise for an upcoming gala. He insists on nothing short of spectacular."

"Of course," I reply, pulse quickening. "I specialize in spectacular." I want to squeal like a high school girl. *Yes, yes, yes!*

"Excellent. Mr. Bennett will expect no less. Details will follow. Prepare to exceed expectations, Ms. Greene."

"Always do," I say, but the line is already dead, buzzing with the silence of anticipation. I stand rooted to the sidewalk, the world blurring around me. This is it—the break I so desperately need.

Not only could this booking get me close to

paying off my start-up business loans, but it could open up doors to better venues.

Higher-paying clients.

Success and stability.

I can't stop the grin that breaks across my face.

I'm going to plan the hell out of this gala.

two

. . .

Alex

I STAND at the edge of the murmuring crowd, a flute of champagne teetering forgotten between my fingers. Sharp jabs about my perpetually single status assault me from all sides. Well-meaning, but they sting all the same.

I'm weary of this conversation—the same one that's been gnawing at me for years. It's as though my success is nothing without a partner to flaunt.

"Alex, you've got everything—a woman's touch is all that's missing in your life," my sister prods with a nudge that's less playful and more pointed.

"Maybe he's just too picky," chimes in my

brother, before he laughs like he's cracked the funniest joke of the evening.

Their barbs cling to my skin. I resist the urge to rub away their expectations along with the irritation that comes with them.

Why is my love life—or lack thereof—anyone's business but my own?

It's not that I don't want a woman. I just haven't found that *one* yet.

Granted, I don't know how I'll know that I've found *the one*, only that somehow I will.

I'll just *know*.

I think.

Fuck, I don't know.

I scowl.

My sister makes another serious remark wrapped up in a teasing tone, but before I can conjure up a retort, my attention snags on something—or rather, *someone*—far more captivating.

There's a goddess standing amidst the opulence of the gala, a striking contrast to the sea of tailored suits and designer gowns. I watch in awe as she holds her hand up to an earpiece, her lips moving urgently.

Those lips...holy fuck. They're wet and glistening with red gloss.

Like ripe cherries...

My cock twitches in my pants as my eyes rove over her heart-shaped face.

Green eyes, dark hair that flows down her curvy back. My fingers twitch at the dip in her back, her waist.

She's all curves and confidence, her dress hugging every inch of her like it was painted on just for her.

Her every move radiates efficiency, the way she glides across the floor with purpose, orchestrating the night's events with an invisible hand.

She must be the event planner I hired. Fucking hell, had I know this sweet thing would be orgaizing everything, I might have taken a more active role in the planning of this evening.

My eyes trace the length of her legs, the swell of her breasts beneath the fabric, a primal appreciation coursing through my veins.

A surge of something darker curls within me, possessive and immediate.

I *want* her.

The intensity of this sudden desire takes me by surprise, the ferocity unlike anything I've felt before. And it's not just her body that has me entranced—it's *everything* about her.

She has this confidence but also this innocence about her.

I tear my eyes off her long enough to pull up my emails. I quickly locate the one with the details about tonight and find what I'm looking for.

Charlotte Greene. Goes by Charlie.

Charlie.

Even her name feels like a puzzle piece clicking into place—a perfect match for the enigmatic woman who now holds my rapt attention.

My heart pounds a rhythm that syncs with the steps she takes, each one echoing the growing need taking root deep within me.

"Excuse me," I say, abandoning my glass on a passing tray with a clatter. The chatter of my siblings fades behind me as I navigate the crowd, intent on one thing.

Get to *her.*

Every instinct tells me what I'm about to do is reckless, but caution has no place here—not when every fiber of my being demands that I know her.

I close the distance between us, my stride confident. She's a vision against the backdrop of opulence—her curves wrapped in professionalism, yet screaming to be unwrapped, and I'm like a kid at Christmas.

"Busy night, huh?" My voice is silk over steel as I lean casually against the marble pillar beside her.

Charlie doesn't miss a beat, her eyes flicking to

mine for just a fraction of a second before returning to her clipboard.

"You're handling everything beautifully. It's rare to see someone so...dedicated."

It's as if she finally realizes who I am because her eyes flick back up to mine and she apologizes, "I'm so sorry, Mr. Bennet. I was engrossed in triple-checking the menu."

"Alex," I correct her smoothly, letting my name hang between us like an invitation. "And triple-checking?" I chuckle softly. "Sounds like you're as much of a perfectionist as I am."

Her lips twitch, almost smiling, but she maintains her professionalism. "It's important to me that everything goes perfectly at these events."

I nod, appreciating her diligence and the slight flush on her

cheeks as she speaks. Her commitment is admirable, and it only fuels my curiosity about her.

"Can I do something for you?" she asks, all business.

"Something like that." I flash a grin, but it fades as she remains unmoved, unimpressed. "Have dinner with me."

The words slip out, more command than request.

She blinks and looks startled, but then she

quickly recovers, her veneer of professionalism falling back over her face. "Mr. Bennett—Alex— thank you, but I don't mix business with pleasure. It's unprofessional."

My heart falls, and something coils tight in my chest. Panic—an unfamiliar and loathsome sensation—grips me.

I can't let her walk away. The thought alone is intolerable.

"I'll pay you," I blurt out.

Her eyebrows shoot up, and I wince. "Dammit, that came out wrong," I quickly ammend.

"I think I should go—" she turns to walk away, and I damn near have a heart attack.

"Wait," I say, and there's an edge of desperation in my voice I barely recognize."Hear me out."

She pauses, eyebrows raised, waiting.

And I don't know what the fuck comes over me, but I say the craziest, stupidest thing I can think of in a last-ditch bid to keep her from walking away.

I just need to buy more time with her, and I don't give a fuck how I go about doing that.

"Be my fake girlfriend." If possible, her eyes, framed by those thick, beautiful lashes, get even wider. "It's not what you think," I go on. I'm babbling now, and it's pathetic, but fuck, it's the effect this woman apparently has on me.

"It's...strategic. For appearances. My family—they won't stop giving me shit about not having a girlfriend."

"Fake girlfriend?" Her voice is incredulous, skeptical. "Why would I—"

"Because I'll pay you a lot," I interrupt, urgency bleeding into my words. "Enough to make any financial worries disappear."

Charlie's expression is unreadable for a moment that stretches too long. Then, slowly, she lowers her clipboard. "How much are we talking?"

"Name your price," I say without hesitation.

"Playing someone's girlfriend isn't exactly in my job description," she says, but there's a new note in her voice.

Thank fuck, she's considering it.

"Consider it a side gig. One that pays exceptionally well." Hope surges through my veins. "What do you say?"

She studies me, her gaze intense and probing. I hold my breath, waiting, needing her to say yes.

Not for the sake of quieting my family, but because the desire to have her by my side—even under false pretenses—has become a craving I can't ignore.

"Fine," she finally says, and relief crashes into

me like a wave. "But we set clear terms. This is strictly business."

"Strictly business," I echo, a victorious smile curling my lips.

"Starting now," she adds firmly, extending her hand.

I take it, and a jolt of electricity shoots up my arm from the contact. My cock shoots a spurt of precum from my tip. I feel it stain the inside of my pants.

Christ Almighty, what this curvy beauty does to me.

No way in hell this is strictly business.

Because Charlie is *the one*.

I know it.

three

. . .

Charlie

I FLICK off the light and sink into the darkness of my living room, the only illumination a sliver of moonlight that slashes across the hardwood floor.

My heart is a trapped bird in a cage of ribs, fluttering wild with every replay of tonight's gala in my head. I should be asleep, but the echo of *his* voice, deep and persuasive, keeps me awake.

The offer was ludicrous. Play the doting girlfriend to Alexander Bennett, billionaire CEO with a touch that could sear through silk.

But desperation has a funny way of painting

lies in shades of necessary evil. Debt doesn't care about morals.

So, I agreed—against the screaming protests of my conscience.

But why me? The question nags at me. There were women at that gala who dripped diamonds and sophistication, yet Alex's blue gaze, sharp as cut glass, fixed on *me*. His choice feels like a riddle wrapped in a mystery inside an enigma, and I'm without a cipher.

Do I scream desperate?

I pull the throw blanket tighter around my shoulders, seeking warmth against the chill thought. I've tried so hard to craft a veneer of confidence. I certainly hope I don't look like a desperate little girl. Because I *am* a confident, successful woman.

I have to keep telling myself that.

No matter how absurd or reckless Alex's proposal was, I have to admire it. That's the kind of confidence money breeds. And Alex Bennett reeks of it—the power, the potency.

But there's something else, too, an undercurrent I can't quite name. His eyes had held mine a beat too long, a stormy sea trying to pull me under. He wants this charade, sure. Yet, why do I get the feeling he's grasping at something more?

"Damn it," I mutter, dragging a hand through my dark hair. It's crazy. Men like him don't fall for women like me—they use them as arm candy, as a means to an end.

But even as I think it, I remember the possessive curl of his fingers around my wrist, branding me with unspoken claims.

A shiver goes through me, and I feel my panties get wet.

I scowl.

No! No, no, no, no, no! No, you don't! I scream at my body. *Don't you dare go getting all hot over the sexy billionaire. This is just business. That's it!*

I'm in over my head. I've agreed to lie, to parade around on the arm of a man who probably doesn't do anything without an ulterior motive.

And I *will not* allow myself to fall for him.

Because it's all a sham.

I have to remember that.

***

Alex

I can't sleep.

Every time I close my eyes I see *her.*

Her green eyes framed by thick lashes.

That dark hair cascading down her back.

Those curves.

Fucking hell, those curves.

My fingers twitch even now, yearning to feel her waist in between them.

I imagine cupping the globes of her breasts, that sweet fucking ass.

My cock is rock hard and leaking at the thought.

I know I fucked up. Offering her this fake relationship—it was a panic move.

I want her—fucking hell, I want her in every way a man can want a woman.

The intensity of this desire feels like a betrayal to my usual control, a break in the armor I've spent years fortifying.

What the hell did she do to me? Her professional demeanor, the way she carries herself, it's like she's untouchable.

And that just makes me want to touch her more.

I roll over in bed, punching my pillow in frustration. Every time I think of her agreeing so reluctantly, something twists inside me.

I don't want her to think this is fake.

Because it's real dammit. These feelings I have for you, they're realer than anything I've ever felt.

I know it's fast, but I also know that I don't give a flying fuck.

I'm not one to sit and overanalyze the fuck out of something. If something feels right, I go with it.

And sticking my dick so far up Charlie's cunt that she'll never remember another man's name let alone his face is what's going to feel right.

My cock twitches thinking about her pussy.

What it looks like…

What is *tastes* like…

I bet she's sweet as hell.

Dammit!

A jet of precum shoots from my tip, and I can't take it anymore.

I fist my hard cock and start stroking it up and down as I imagine Charlie naked.

Under me, writhing in ecstasy. Her eyes locked onto mine, heavy with lust, whispering my name like a sacred mantra.

The fantasy alone is enough to drive me wild, the thrill of conquest mingling with an unfamiliar urge to protect and possess.

I keep her image at the forefront of my thoughts. Every stroke is punctuated with the memory of her smile, the way she bit her lip when something amused her, the husky sound of her laughter.

It's maddening how vividly I can recall her every detail after just one night.

Maybe that's what genuine desire does to a man—brands every glance and gesture into his brain, making it impossible for him to think of anything else.

I groan as my climax builds, the culmination of all these pent-up desires about to explode.

With every pulse and throb, I imagine it's Charlie underneath me, not just my own hand.

I picture plunging into her depths, feeling her clench around me, hearing her gasp out my name in a mix of shock and pleasure.

"Fuck!" The word rips from my throat as I come hard, my seed spilling over my fingers in hot, white streaks.

I fall back onto my bed, panting heavily.

A surge of emptiness washes over me. It's hollowness, a craving unsatisfied, because it wasn't her wrapped around me.

It wasn't her breath hot on my skin.

The room feels colder suddenly, the sheets too smooth, too empty. I swing my legs over the side of the bed, resting my head in my hands.

The idea of using her as a decoy to satisfy the press and my ever-interfering family fills me with shame.

How the fuck could I even suggest that when all I want is to hold her in my arms and cherish her forever?

I've got to make this right.

But I don't even know where to begin to start.

four

. . .

Charlie

MY PHONE BUZZES against the glass tabletop, its vibration a sharp, insistent thing. I glance at the screen—Alexander Bennett's name glows back at me.

Heat crawls up my neck as I swipe to answer.

"Charlie," Alex's voice is a stroke of velvet over the line, dark and promising. "Dinner tonight? I thought it might be beneficial for us to...acquaint ourselves further."

"Sure," I reply, my practicality wrestling with the flutter in my stomach. "What time?"

"I'll pick you up at eight."

There's something about the way he asserts control, even over simple logistics, that sends a shiver dancing down my spine.

The rest of my afternoon blurs into a haze of anticipation and anxiety. Each passing hour tightens the knot in my stomach, not solely from nerves but also an unfamiliar excitement.

I try not too fuss too much with my appearance because I am *not* trying to impress him.

It's fake, after all.

———

Alex

Charlotte Greene, with her sharp wit and even sharper curves, has been a relentless distraction since the day I first laid eyes on her. She's all I fucking see, all I can think about.

My cock is perpetually hard thinking about it, but it's more than just the physical sensations she elicits in me.

It's the way I feel when I look into her beautiful green eyes.

Like coming home.

I spend the afternoon in meetings, but my thoughts keep drifting to her—her dark hair falling perfectly around her face, her green eyes that seem to pierce through the façade I wear for everyone else. She's a challenge, a beautiful enigma wrapped in caution and sensuality.

By 7:45 p.m., I'm pulling up to her apartment in my sleek black limo. My driver idles on the curb as I step out and adjust my cufflinks. I also smooth back my hair, preparing to see her again.

The anticipation coils tight in my chest as I ring her doorbell.

Charlie

The sound of the doorbell echoes through my small apartment, a stark reminder of the evening that lies ahead. I take one last glance in the mirror, smoothing down my dress and taking a deep breath to calm the fluttering in my chest.

It's just dinner, I remind myself. *Just a part of the charade to keep the gossip mills at bay and protect his reputation.*

I open the door, and I'm momentarily breath-less. Alex stands there, every inch the epitome of a dark prince from some erotic fairytale.

His presence commands the space, his eyes immediately capturing mine in a gaze I find hard to break.

"Good evening, Charlie," he says, his voice a low rumble that seems to vibrate through me as his dark gaze rakes over me, lingering on my curves.

He extends his arm, and without thinking, I place my hand in his. His fingers close around mine with possessive warmth.

As we walk to his limousine, every step feels charged. The air between us crackles with an elec-tric current that pulls me closer into his orbit. Despite the cool evening air, his nearness envelops me in a warmth that's as intoxicating as the finest whiskey.

I shake my head.

Get ahold of yourself, Charlie.

———

Alex

The soft clink of her heels against the pavement is like a metronome to my rising desire. As we slide into the limo, our thighs brush, a simple touch that sends adrenaline spiking through my veins.

I want to explore every inch of her—want to break down the barriers she puts up.

In the dim light of the limousine, her eyes look greener, almost ethereal. "You look stunning tonight," I murmur, allowing the truth of my words to hover in the air between us.

She flushes, a delightful pink creeping up her cheeks. "Thank you, Alex," she replies, her voice steady but with an undercurrent of something else —something like anticipation.

I lean closer, my hand finding hers again. The contact is deliberate, reaffirming the silent promise I made to myself—to have her, wholly and completely. My thumb caresses the back of her hand, a seemingly innocent gesture that carries the weight of all my unspoken desires.

The limo pulls away from the curb smoothly, gliding through the city streets as we sit wrapped in a cocoon of tension and luxury. The quiet intimacy of the space amplifies every breath, every slight movement.

Charlie shifts slightly, turning to face me more directly. "So, Alex, what's the agenda for tonight?"

Her tone is casual, and professional that she is, she's direct and to the point..

I smile, a slow, deliberate curve of my lips. "No agenda," I say softly. "Just two people enjoying each other's company." The words hang between us, laden with meaning. I watch as her gaze flickers with a mix of curiosity and wariness.

The car stops at a red light, and I seize the moment. Leaning in closer, I drop my voice to a whisper, "And maybe discovering things about each other that could surprise us both."

Her breath catches, and the subtle scent of her perfume—a mix of vanilla and something undeniably spicy—fills the space between us.

It's intoxicating, *addictive*.

Her eyes hold mine, a silent battle of wills occurring in the depth of those verdant pools.

"Yes, we should definitely know a few facts about each other," she finally says, and my heart falls.

She's looking at this like an assignment.

And of course she is. She thinks it's all fake.

I'm *paying* her for Christ's sake.

I sit back in the limo and fall silent.

Damn it all to hell.

five

. . .

Charlie

THE RESTAURANT IS a study in shadows and whispers, intimacy carved out in mahogany and candlelight. Alex dominates the space across from me, his presence an indomitable force that pulls at every sense.

"Let's come up with our story," I suggest as I swirl the wine in my glass, watching the red liquid cling to the crystal. "If we're going to convince everyone we're dating, we need a solid story."

"Okay," he says, though he seems less than thrilled about the prospect.

In fact, he's been brooding ever since the limo ride.

I look at him curiously. Just what's up with him?

My heart falls. Am I really *that* boring?

I focus on the task at hand. "It has to be plausible but romantic enough to satisfy the skeptics."

"Romantic..." he muses, drumming his fingers on the table.

"An event," I start, my mind ticking through scenarios with practiced ease, "One of my planning, naturally. You're there, not expecting much beyond business networking."

"Until I see you," he interjects smoothly, blue eyes locking onto mine.

"Exactly," I say, a shiver running down my spine, though I fight to keep my composure. "Our eyes meet across the room. There's an instant...something. A connection neither of us can ignore."

"Compelling," he says, his gaze tracing the contours of my face as if committing each detail to memory. "And then?"

"Then, you approach me. Confident. Direct." My voice drops a notch, mirroring the intensity in his eyes. "You're not accustomed to waiting for what you want."

"True," he acknowledges, a smile playing on those full lips. "I insist on taking you out. You're reluctant at first, but eventually, you concede."

"Because deep down," I add, the character I'm creating bleeding into my own reality, "I don't want to resist the pull between us."

"Perfect," he pronounces, the word a low growl of approval.

We delve deeper into our fiction, crafting each moment with care, unaware of how closely the lie entwines with a truth unspoken.

Alex's gaze lingers on me, unblinking, as if he's trying to decrypt my every expression. It's unnerving but enthralling—like being studied by a predator that has chosen its prey.

"Tell me something real," he says suddenly, his voice threading through the restaurant's hum like a velvet ribbon.

I falter, caught off-guard. "Real?" I echo, my practical nature grappling with the intimacy of the request.

"Anything," he prompts, leaning closer, the table between us the only barrier.

There's a vulnerability in his blue eyes, a crack in the armor of the billionaire CEO who's accustomed to scripted interactions and calculated moves. I relent, letting him glimpse behind my professional façade.

"When I was little, I wanted to be an astronaut," I confess, the admission feeling both insignificant and monumental under his intense scrutiny.

"Reaching for the stars," he muses. And then he smiles, "Yes, I can see that."

His words wrap around me, binding, *possessive*. The air shifts, charged with something.

"What about you?" I ask him.

He stares at me so long I start to wonder if I've offended him.

———

Alex

The question catches me off guard—a simple inquiry, yet it feels like a test.

What can I reveal to her that isn't already public knowledge, something personal that doesn't expose too much vulnerability?

My fingers tap rhythmically against the glass of my wine, the red liquid swirling like the tumultuous thoughts in my mind.

"I used to write," I confess, my voice steadier than I feel. "Poetry, mostly. It was a way to escape the pressures of my family's expectations."

Her eyebrows lift, a hint of surprise coloring her expression. It's satisfying, this small victory of revealing an unexpected facet of myself. "Really? I wouldn't have pegged you for a poet."

I chuckle, the sound more genuine than I intend. "Few do. It was a long time ago." I pause, considering how much more to share. "It was about capturing moments, emotions...things I found hard to express aloud."

Her eyes soften, and she leans in slightly, her curiosity piqued. "Do you still write?" she asks, her voice tinged with a mix of hope and something else —something I don't dare hope for.

I hesitate, the truth knotted in my throat. "Not for years," I admit, feeling a sharp pang of loss for the part of me that reveled in versed expressions.

But looking into Charlie's eyes, lines flow through my head unbidden.

I could write volumes about *her*.

Charlotte nods thoughtfully, her gaze not leaving mine. "It's never too late to pick it up again," she says softly, the encouragement in her voice warming something inside me that had long been cold.

And I know now that I'm completely fucking in love with this curvy beauty.

———

The drive home is silent, thick with the residue of unfulfilled craving. My cock is so fucking hard, it's all I can do to keep from dragging Charlie's sexy self over here and pulling her onto my lap.

I want to grind myself against her and kiss her lips, her neck, that delicious fucking cleavage that's been taunting me all night.

When the limo purrs to a stop outside her place, I adjust myself as discreetly as I can before getting out to walk her to her door.

"Goodnight, Charlie," I murmur. I want to kiss her, but something tells me she won't be receptive to it.

Not now

"Goodnight, Alex," I replies with a smile that makes my dick ache. She steps inside, and the click of the closing door severs our connection.

I make my way back to the limo and throw myself into the backseat.

"Drive!" I snap at my driver as I roll up the partition that separates him from me.

I don't need anyone witnessing my insanity as I

press my face into the seat where Charlie sat moments ago.

I inhale the lingering scent of her perfume mixed with the leather as I unzip my trousers and free my aching cock.

A stream of precum leaks from my tip. I smear it all over myself and begin to stroke.

Fuck, being so close to Charlie all night yet unable to touch her…it was torture.

"Charlie," I groan into the silence, her name a talisman invoking visions of what could be.

My hand moves in fervent strokes, chasing release as I fantasize about possessing her completely, utterly.

All while I sniff where her sweet ass sat like a deranged lunatic.

My climax builds swiftly, a crescendo of lust and frustration fueled by the electric images of Charlotte's curvaceous body, her green eyes veiled with desire in my mind's eye. I picture her lips parted, the sound of her breath hitched in expectation.

My strokes become more erratic, more desperate as I imagine sliding into her heat, feeling her clench around me.

"Fuck, Charlie…" My voice breaks on her name, the intensity of my fantasy overwhelming.

As the tension coils tighter within me, each stroke fans the flames higher, and I'm close—so damn close—to spilling myself while lost in thoughts of her. The imagined sensation of her soft thighs wrapped around my hips pushes me over the edge.

With a guttural groan, my release crashes over me in powerful waves. I come hard, hot streaks of semen splashing against my hand and the leather seat beneath me.

My breath is heavy, ragged, as I come down from the high, the reality of my situation sinking in with the cooling of my skin.

What the fuck am I doing?

I clean myself up with a handful of tissues from the compartment beside me, each wipe a harsh reminder of how dangerously close I am to losing control around her.

The frustration is still there, simmering beneath the post-orgasmic haze.

But it's not just sexual—it's emotional, this unsettling desire to claim her as *mine*.

In all ways possible.

six

. . .

Alex

THE CLINK of fine china and the murmur of elite conversation blend into a symphony of high society, but I hear none of it. Not with Charlie by my side.

She's a vision in crimson silk that hugs her curves like a sinner's promise, dark hair cascading over bare shoulders. As she glides beside me, every eye shifts, drawn by her confidence.

The raw fucking sexiness of her that has me ready to cream my pants right here and now.

I can't help but swell with pride, knowing she's here with me.

But as gazes linger too long, appreciation turning lecherous, my blood simmers. They see her exterior, not all of her the way I do. They don't deserve even a glance, yet they feast.

My hands ball into fists.

"Alex?" Charlie's voice cuts through the haze of my jealousy, sharp, professional. "Shall we mingle?"

"Of course," I say, placing a hand possessively at the small of her back, asserting silently to everyone here.

She's with me.

As we circulate, every man's nod is courteous but calculating, their eyes betraying the greediness of their intentions.

I lean in closer to Charlie, marking my territory with a touch that brooks no argument. She stiffens under my hand, and I know I've overstepped.

"Alex, you're holding onto me pretty tight there," she says, a teasing lilt to her words, but her green eyes are serious. "Relax, this isn't a real date."

"Isn't it?" I challenge, voice low, the words for her alone. "If this were real, I wouldn't let anyone else look at you. You'd be mine, completely."

Her breath catches, and for a moment, there's a flicker of something more than our charade. But then she masks it with a practiced smile and steps away, reclaiming her independence.

"Then it's a good thing this is just for show," she replies, but the tremor in her voice betrays the tension between us—a tension that feels anything but fake.

Charlie's retreat isn't just a step back physically. It feels like a chasm opening between us, filled with all the unspoken words and simmering tension.

I force myself to loosen my grip, but my mind is racing, my instincts screaming to pull her back, to claim her as mine in every way that matters. Hell, I want to fuck her right here and now in front of everyone just so everyone will know she's mine. At the same time, I can't bear the thought of anyone else seeing her body.

It's *mine* alone.

The evening drags on, each minute stretching longer than the last as I watch her navigate the room with me by her side.

Her laughter rings out, light and carefree, a stark contrast to the tumult brewing inside me.

She's a vision, effortlessly charming everyone she speaks to, her curvy figure wrapped in a dress that clings just right, accentuating every line and curve that drives me to distraction. The fabric whispers against her skin with every move she makes, and it's doing a number on my frayed self-control.

Every laugh she shares, every hand she shakes

—it feels like a tiny betrayal, though I know it's irrational. My jaw clenches each time another man leans in to whisper something meant to be charming, hoping to capture a sliver of her attention. Their eyes travel across her form with hungry admiration, and it fuels a fire within me that burns all the more fiercely each time I catch their covetous glances.

I want to roar, to unleash the primal urge simmering just beneath my civilized veneer, to tell them she is off limits. But instead, I channel this furious energy into a practiced smile as I draw her closer once more, my arm slipping around her waist with proprietary ease.

"Enjoying yourself?" I murmur into her ear, my lips barely brushing the delicate shell.

She tilts her head slightly, acknowledging my proximity with a shiver that she tries to mask as indifference. "I am here to support your business interests, Alex," she replies firmly, yet there's a warmth there that wasn't present before—a warmth that belies her controlled exterior.

The evening wears on, each tick of the clock a loud echo in my simmering mind. Every conversation feels like another test of my restraint, every polite smile a challenge to my claim over her.

It's an exquisite sort of torture, seeing her so

alive in the elements of this glittering throng, knowing she's untouchable and yet undeniably mine for the night. The contradiction fuels a dangerous thrill down my spine.

As the night draws to a close, and we prepare to leave, I feel a sense of urgency pulsating within me.

"Let me take you home," I demand.

"That's okay—" She starts to protest, but I grab her hand. I'm having none of that.

A shock goes through me as I feel the soft warmth of her skin against mine. I pull her slightly behind me as we make our way out.

Her fingers tense in mine, but she doesn't pull away.

Once we're safely ensconced in the back seat of my limo, the privacy feels like a sudden drop from a high cliff into deep water. My voice is rough with barely-contained desire as I turn to face her, our knees touching in the dim light of the car interior. "Charlie, I—"

She holds up a hand, her eyes searching mine in the half-light. "Alex, we need to set some boundaries," she says softly, yet there's an iron undercurrent to her voice that commands my full attention.

I grit my teeth, frustration boiling inside me. I want to object, to pull her into my arms and erase all the formalities with a kiss.

But instead, I exhale slowly, trying to cage the beast of possessiveness roaring in my chest. "Tell me," I manage to say through clenched teeth.

"Tonight was too much," she admits, tucking a stray lock of hair behind her ear—a nervous gesture that doesn't escape me. "You were...too intense. I get we want to make it believable, but maybe try not to put off such jealous vibes? I don't think that's such a good look for your image. I'm thinking it should be more the 'happy couple' vibes for what you're trying to achieve, don't you?"

I grit my teeth together. Damn it, she's right—if this really was fake dating, that is, and of course that's all it is to her because that's how my dumb ass presented all this.

Something raw twists in my guts. It's more than playacting, more than a charade for the benefit of prying eyes. I'm out of my depth here, drowning in a sea of emotions that have no right to exist in our agreement.

"I know," I concede with a nod, the word gritted out between teeth that hardly want to let it escape. "It's just...hard. Watching them look at you like that. I would never be okay with men ogling my girl like that."

Her gaze softens, and those damn beautiful eyes pierce through my heart. "Alex," she starts, her voice a soothing balm that threatens to undo me, "I'm used to it."

I damn near see red. She's used to it?

But then her voice grounds me, "But I can take care of myself. And when we're out in public, I'm yours."

I know she's speaking professionally, but hearing Charlie say she's mine soothes the beast inside me that was struggling to break free at the thought that my woman is used to men leering at her like she's a piece of meat.

Her reassurance flickers through me like a warm flame, calming the storm that had been raging within. The car's smooth motion and the privacy of the darkened interior allow me to regain some semblance of control over my emotions.

As we glide through the city streets, I can't help but glance at her intermittently, watching how the streetlights play across her features.

Each time I look at her, I feel that now-familiar pull—like a tide drawn irresistibly to the moon. It nudges me closer to her until our shoulders brush slightly.

Charlie doesn't move away. Instead, she lets out a soft sigh, tilting her head to rest against my shoulder. The simple gesture unravels me more than any heated exchange could.

In this quiet space between heartbeats, something shifts.

And when we pull up outside her apartment, it takes everything in me not to haul her to my chest and never let her go.

My eyes watch her as she enters the drab building that's not good enough for a woman like her.

She belongs back at my penthouse with me where I can spoil her and give her everything her heart desires.

If only I can make her see that.

seven

. . .

Charlie

HEAT COILS in my belly as I step into the grand ballroom, clinging to Alex's arm. The room glimmers with crystal chandeliers and a hunger that mirrors my own—a hunger I tamp down because this—*us*—it's not real.

"Relax, Charlie," Alex whispers, his breath warm against my ear, sending shivers down my spine. He squeezes my hand, a gesture meant to reassure but it only ignites the fire inside me.

I'm playing a role, I remind myself sternly. Eye candy on the arm of Alexander Bennett, billionaire

CEO, at a charity ball—it's all business, even if my body screams otherwise.

His suit hugs his muscular frame, the sight commanding as much attention as the wealth whispering through the air.

"Smile for the cameras," he murmurs, his lips brushing against my temple in a move so possessive, every nerve ending sizzles with awareness. His blue eyes lock onto mine, piercing and intense.

"Always," I manage, my voice doesn't waver, but my heart does—a traitorous thing pounding in my chest.

We glide across the floor, mingling with guests, laughter and light swirling around us. But the pull between us is a current too strong to ignore. With each brush of his fingertips along the small of my back, restraint threads thinner, my professional facade cracking under his touch.

"Enjoying the evening?" he asks, tilting his head to study me.

And that's the thing that's killing me. Alex would totally make an amazing boyfriend. He's always checking on me. He's attentive, gorgeous, possessive.

I can only imagine what he's like in the bedroom—

Nope! Nope! Nope! Nope! I scream at myself. Do *not* go there!

"Immensely," I lie, the word tasting sour on my tongue. I'm lost in the charade, in him—afraid of how much I want it to be true.

Then, amidst applause for a successful bid, he turns to me, his gaze burning with something forbidden.

Before I can protest, Alex's mouth crashes against mine, and holy fucking moly.

I freeze. His kiss…it's demanding. He's claiming me in front of everyone.

The world fades away, leaving only the sensation of his lips, firm yet hungry against mine. I'm caught in the storm of him, and for a heartbeat, I kiss him back, drowning in the delusion of us.

It's raw, it's public, and it's not part of the plan.

But then reality comes crashing back in, sharp and stinging.

This is all just an act.

Or at least, it's supposed to be.

I shove him back, my chest heaving in a cocktail of rage and desire. "Kissing me? Here? That wasn't part of the deal, Alex."

His blue eyes smolder, undeterred by my fury. "It felt right," he says, voice low, every word laced with that same possessiveness that commands boardrooms.

"Stop it. Just stop." I can't let him see the truth, can't admit how his lips seared against mine kindle something that terrifies me. My heart betrays me, thudding with a yearning that feels too much like love—love that has no place in our fabricated romance.

"Charlie," he starts, taking a step closer, but I'm retreating already, my heels clicking a staccato retreat across the marble floor. The space between us stretches taut, filled with electric tension.

"Alex, don't," I warn, my voice trembling despite my best efforts to sound stern. I've fallen into a dangerous game, my own emotions the price.

I run from him, from the humiliation burning in my cheeks, from the palpable want coiling tight within me.

I can feel a hundred gazes on me. I'm completely breaking script, but I don't care. No doubt it's going to be all over the news about Alex's "girlfriend" running out on him like a crazed lunatic, but I don't care.

All I care about is gaining back some semblance of self-preservation.

"Charlotte!" Alex calls after me, but I don't stop.

Each step echoes my heartbeat, fast and frenzied, as I escape into the anonymity of the night.

Because if I stay with Alex, my heart is doomed.

And it will utterly crush me when he ends it.

eight

. . .

Alex

I SPRINT AFTER CHARLIE, my heart pounding in my chest with every determined step.

She's fast, but my longer strides close the gap between us until I'm just a breath away. With a gentle but firm grip, I catch her wrist, spinning her around to face me. Her green eyes flash with surprise, then something fiercer.

"Charlie," I pant, not just from the chase but from the surge of emotion that tightens my throat.

"That wasn't part of our agreement!" she shouts at me. "Kissing me, it wasn't...it wasn't..." she babbles, her furious gaze clouded with tears of anger.

"I only asked you to be my fake date because you turned down a real one!" I tell vehemently, my truth spilling out in a rush.

Her eyes widen, and for a moment, she's speechless—a rare victory for me.

"I'm infatuated with you! No, wait. Infatuated doesn't even begin to cover it," I confess, my voice raw with honesty. "I'm obsessed with you, Charlie. From the moment I first saw you...I can't stop thinking about you."

The air between us crackles, charged with tension and unspoken desires.

Her beautiful chest is heaving up and down.

I'm breathing heavily.

Our eyes lock.

My eyes flick down to her puffy pink lips...

Then, our bodies collide.

My hands roam over her curves, feeling the heat of her through the fabric of her clothes, while hers tangle in my hair, pulling me closer.

"Alex," she gasps, and that's all the consent I need.

With a growl of possessive need, I claim her mouth with mine, devouring her sweet taste. She tastes like cherries and innocence and sin wrapped all into one delicious cocktail.

I don't even know where the fuck we're at, but I maneuver us into an alcove. I think we're in a motherfucking alley, but I don't care.

I pull her dress up and cup the delicious globes of her ass as I lift her. Her legs wrap around me, and I put my hand between us only long enough to free my aching dick.

My cock prods at her dripping wet hole, and then I'm pushing into her.

Mother*fucker*, she's tight! "How is this pussy so damn tight?" I grit out.

"Because it's my first time," she gasps.

My blood boils with desire and possession at her words. "Oh fuck, baby, don't tell me that. I'm already going crazy over you. You want me to go completely insane? Do you mean to tell me my cock is the first one to ever be in this sweet thing?"

Charlie gasps as I go an inch futher, her arms wrapping around me tightly as she manages a shaky, "Uh-huh."

"Then know this," I grab her chin and force her to look at me, "I'm going to be the *only* cock ever inside this sweet pussy. You hear me?"

"Yes," she whimpers as her pussy pulsates around me. Holy hell, is she already coming?

"That's a good girl," I praise her. "You come on this dick on you want because it's all yours, baby."

I thrust the rest of the way inside her, burying all my inches as deep as I can go and as I take what she willingly offers, I know I'm claiming more than just her body.

I'm marking her soul—just like she's marked mine.

The realization she's untouched sends a primal thrill through me, and I'm gentler now, worshiping every inch of her with my lips and tongue as I move within her.

"God, Charlie, you're so perfect," I groan, mesmerized by the way her body stretches and yields to mine. "So damn hot... all these curves...made just for me."

Her moans are my undoing, and as I stroke my cock in and out of her delicious pussy, I lean down to whisper fiercely against her ear, "I'll never use a condom, Charlie. *Never*. Never want anything between us."

"Alex!" she screams my name, and that's my undoing. I feel my load rocketing up my stalk, and then I'm flooding her pussy with my seed.

I come so much, there's no way in hell I'm not going to get her pregnant, and that's alright with me because this woman is going to be my wife.

"Every sweet inch of you belongs to me," I tell her, and I seal that vow with a deep, searing kiss that promises eternity.

epilogue

. . .

Five years later

Charlie

THE SUN DIPS below the horizon, casting a soft glow through the large windows of our penthouse. I watch our twin boys, their laughter mingling with the clink of toys, an echo of pure joy that fills the spacious living room.

After that night that Alex chased after me and admitted the truth, we became a real couple, and it wasn't shortly after that we were married.

And true to his word, Alex has *never* used a condom with me.

My event planning business took off in full swing with the full support of my billionaire husband.

He's still growly and possessive as hell and insists on going with me to every event I do to keep other men away from me, but I'm totally okay with that because I'm just as addicted to him as he is to me.

Alex's arms encircle me from behind, his lips grazing the sensitive skin at the nape of my neck. My entire body trembles, and I hear the low growl in his throat as he presses his hard cock against my ass.

I squeeze my thighs together to try to ease the sudden ache that's bloomed between them.

"Boys," Alex calls out with authority softened by affection, "time for bed."

I turn within his embrace to face him, his piercing blue eyes locking onto mine. "Let me tuck them in," I whisper, my heart swelling with love for the life we've built.

"Of course, beautiful." His voice is a seductive promise.

Minutes later, after kisses goodnight and a short goodnight story, our boys are fast asleep. I return to find Alex, lounging like a panther on the prowl, his tailored suit replaced by the shadows and contours of our dimly lit bedroom.

"Come here," he demands, a hint of possessiveness lacing his tone.

My feet carry me toward him, magnetized by the intensity of his gaze. He watches every sway of my hips, like a hunter focused solely on his prey.

When I reach him, his hands roam over my curves, mapping the territory he claims as his own.

"Alex," I gasp as his fingers trace the hem of my silk nightgown, his touch igniting a flame that only burns hotter between us every year.

"Charlie," he growls back, and there's no mistaking the raw desire in his voice. It's dark and heady, filled with unspoken promises.

He peels away the fabric barrier, his movements deliberate and unhurried. The cool air kisses my skin, but it's the heat of his stare that sends shivers down my spine. I'm exposed, vulnerable, but in his eyes, I see nothing but worship.

I sink to my knees, the plush carpet cushioning my descent. Alex's anticipation is tangible, a current that connects us. With deliberate slowness, I undo his belt, the metallic click resonating in the charged silence.

"Fuck, wife," he breathes out, a testament to his unraveling control.

"Shh," I soothe, my fingers trailing lower, freeing him from the confines of his boxer briefs. The sight of his arousal, strong and commanding, makes moisture flood between my thighs.

I lean forward, my lips hovering just a breath away from him. Our eyes lock, a silent conversation passing between us—only *I* get to see him this way.

I take him into my mouth.

"Ah, fuck," Alex hisses, his hand tangling in my dark hair, guiding me with unspoken commands.

His taste, the feel of him on my tongue, it's intoxicating. I indulge in the power I wield over him in this moment, the billionaire CEO undone by my touch. My movements are rhythmically intense, each stroke designed to push him closer to the edge.

I know exactly how my husband likes it.

"Charlie," he groans, his voice thick with need. "You're going to make me—"

But I don't let him finish. I double my efforts, chasing the high that comes with bringing him pleasure. It's a dance as old as time, yet with Alex, it feels like a revelation every single time.

"God, yes," he cries out, the possessive grip on my hair tightening.

And then he surrenders to me completely, his body tensing as he spills himself into my mouth.

I savor the moment, the taste of him, the sound of his ragged breathing.

With a growl, he pulls me up and kisses me fiercely as he stabs his still-hard cock deep inside me.

I moan into his mouth, and I know that this—this wild, possessive love—is our forever.

Want a free book from Emma Bray? Go to www.authoremmabray.com.

Keep reading for an excerpt from the next Curvy Girl Romance Short, Curvy Girl for the Mafia Daddy.

Chapter 1

Luca

I'm sitting at my mahogany desk, my fingers steepled as I gaze out at the glittering city lights below. The Rolex on my wrist ticks steadily, each second echoing in the silence of my penthouse office.

The shrill ring of my cell phone cuts through the quiet. I glance at the caller ID. It's Enzo, my most trusted advisor. He wouldn't call at this hour unless it was urgent.

I answer with a curt "What is it?" My voice is gravel.

"Boss, I have some bad news." Enzo's normally stoic tone wavers. "It's about your brother Dante..."

My grip tightens on the phone, jaw clenching. "What about him?"

There's a heavy pause. "He's dead, Boss. Shot outside his home earlier tonight. I'm so sorry."

The words hit me like a punch to the gut. I suck in a sharp breath, a storm of emotions roiling within me—shock, grief, white-hot rage.

My brother, my *blood*, gone just like that. Snuffed out by some cowardly bastard.

"Any leads on who did this?" I growl, my free hand balling into a fist.

"Not yet. But there's something else you should know..." Enzo hesitates. "Dante's wife was also killed. Their son Matteo is alive. He's only five years old."

Matteo. My nephew, now an orphan. The full weight of it hits me. This innocent boy's entire world has just shattered. And as my brother's only living relative, his care now falls to me.

I lean back in my leather chair and close my eyes for a long moment, letting the news sink in. When I open them, they blaze with renewed purpose and determination.

"Enzo, I want a status report within the hour. Mobilize every resource. We're going to find the scum who did this and make them pay." My tone is lethal calm. "And have Matteo brought to the estate immediately. He's under my protection now."

"Yes, Boss. Consider it done."

I end the call and stand, moving to the wall of windows. I press my palm to the cool glass, looking out over my dark kingdom of steel and shadow.

Everything has changed in an instant. But one thing is certain.

I will keep Matteo safe, no matter the cost. And I will rain down unholy vengeance on those who tore our family apart. This I vow, on my brother's blood.

They have no idea the hell that's coming for them.

But then I realize with a start that I don't know the first thing about caring for a child.

I pick up the phone and place a call.

———

The sharp rap of knuckles against wood jolts me from my vengeful musings. I slide my gun into its shoulder holster, schooling my features into an impenetrable mask.

"Enter."

Marco opens the door, revealing a curvaceous young woman clutching a bag, her wide eyes taking in the opulent surroundings. Chestnut curls frame a heart-shaped face—pretty, in a girl-next-door way. Innocence radiates from her like a beacon.

Innocence has no place in my world.

"Boss, this is Dana Johnson. The nanny agency sent her."

I rake her figure with an assessing gaze, noting the way she fidgets under my scrutiny. Nervous. Good. Fear is a useful tool.

"Ms. Johnson." I inject a thread of steel into my voice. "I trust you understand the gravity of this position. Discretion is non-negotiable."

She straightens her spine, meeting my stare head-on. Unexpected. "Of course, Mr. Romano. I'm here for Matteo, nothing else."

Bold little thing. The barest hint of a smile tugs at my mouth before I banish it. "Matteo is the sole focus. You'll be at his beck and call, tending to his every need. I expect your undivided attention on him."

"I wouldn't have it any other way." Conviction rings in her tone. "Childcare is my top priority."

Admirable, but she's naively unaware of the dark undercurrents in this house. In *me*.

I close the distance between us, catching the hitch in her breath when I invade her space. The scent of vanilla and something uniquely feminine invades my nostrils.

"One more thing." My voice is a low purr. "In this house, my word is law. Defy me..." I trail off, letting the unspoken threat hang in the air.

She tips her chin up fractionally, defiance sparking in her eyes. "I don't scare easily, Mr. Romano. And I never back down from a challenge."

Arousal courses through me, fierce and sudden. I want to snap that pretty neck. I want to bury myself inside her until she screams my name.

I do neither.

"Good." I give her a smile devoid of warmth. "Matteo's room is upstairs, third door on the left. Get to work, Ms. Johnson."

She nods, grip tightening on her bag as she walks past me.

Once she's gone, I turn to Marco, eyebrow arched. "Thoughts?"

He shrugs. "Nurturing type. Good with kids. Bit of a spitfire, though."

My eyes gleam, full of wicked promise. "It appears Ms. Johnson needs a lesson in submission."

One I'll greatly enjoy teaching her.

***

Three hours later, and I still can't get the damned nanny out of my head.

What the fuck is it about her?

Those luscious curves…

Those full breasts…

She's got a body on her, that's for sure. But I'm not so shallow that all I care about is looks.

It's something else.

Something I can't quite put my finger on.

I grab my laptop and pull up her file because I'm no idiot. I have a full file made of everyone who enters my domain.

No surprises that way.

Dana Johnson. 24 years old. Graduated top of her class with a degree in early childhood education. Glowing references. Not so much as a parking ticket on her record.

On paper, she's practically a saint. The perfect nanny.

But I saw the flash of defiance in her eyes. The spark of challenge when I laid down the law.

Little Ms. Johnson isn't quite the innocent angel she appears to be.

And I'm just the man to uncover her secrets.

I lean back in my chair, fingers drumming against the polished wood of my desk. I should be focusing on finding Dante's killer, on protecting Matteo, on running my empire.

Instead, I'm obsessing over a goddamn nanny.

I shake my head in disgust. *Get it together, Romano. You're not some horny teenager. You're a fucking king.*

But when I close my eyes, all I see is Dana. That sweet, curvy body. Those defiant eyes. That smart mouth that needs to be put to better use...

Fuuuuck.

I adjust myself, my cock already half-hard just thinking about her. This isn't like me. I'm always in control. Always calling the shots.

But something about her gets under my skin. Makes me want to lose control. To take her and make her *mine* in every way possible.

I need to stay away from her. For both our sakes. She's here for Matteo, not to be my plaything.

But, oh, what a curvy little plaything...

———

Dana

I carefully close the door to Matteo's room, relief washing over me. After a few hours of playing, reading stories, and gently soothing him, the poor little guy is finally asleep. My heart breaks for him. I can't imagine the trauma and confusion he must be feeling.

I lean against the wall for a moment, closing my eyes and just breathing. It's been a whirlwind since I arrived at the Romano estate. The sheer opulence of the place is staggering. And the man who runs it all...

Luca Romano. That name sends a shiver down my spine. He's easily the most intense, intimidating man I've ever met. Those piercing blue eyes seem to see right into my soul, stripping away every defense. And the way his suit clings to that powerful, muscular body...

No. I mentally shake myself. I can't be thinking about my boss that way. Especially not when he's just lost his brother and taken on the enormous responsibility of raising his orphaned nephew. Luca needs my help with Matteo, not my schoolgirl daydreams.

I straighten up, smoothing my skirt. I need to stay focused on what matters—taking the best possible care of that sweet, traumatized little boy. Even if his uncle does make my knees weak and my heart race.

I head downstairs in search of the kitchen, figuring I should familiarize myself with the layout of this massive house.

As I turn the corner into the lavish kitchen, I stop short. Luca is there, his back to me as he faces the marble countertop. His suit jacket is off, revealing the way his crisp white dress shirt stretches across his broad shoulders.

My breath catches in my throat. I didn't expect to run into him so soon. Or for the sight of him to affect me so viscerally.

Get a grip, Dana. He's your boss, not a GQ model.

I clear my throat softly. "Mr. Romano, I didn't mean to disturb you. I was just looking for the kitchen..."

He turns slowly, those ice blue eyes locking onto mine with laser focus. "It's Luca. Mr. Romano was my father."

"Luca," I repeat, my tongue darting out to wet my suddenly dry lips. "I just wanted to let you know that Matteo is asleep. He was understandably upset, but I managed to calm him down."

Luca nods, his gaze never leaving my face. "Good. That's...good."

Is it my imagination, or is his voice a little rougher than before? I suddenly feel too warm, too aware of him as a man, not just my employer.

"I know my way around kids pretty well," I say inanely, desperate to fill the charged silence. "I'm sure in time, with patience and love, Matteo will adjust to his new normal."

"His new normal?" Luca repeats, something dangerous flickering in his eyes. He steps closer, crowding into my space. "There's nothing normal about a five-year-old losing both parents. Nothing normal about having to live with an uncle he barely knows, in a world he has no idea about."

I stand my ground, lifting my chin. "I just meant that with the right support, Matteo can learn to cope and even thrive, despite the tragedy he's facing. He's so young. He's resilient."

Luca scoffs, a harsh sound. "Resilient? He shouldn't have to be resilient. He should have his parents. His innocence."

"You're right," I say softly. "It's not fair. None of this is fair to Matteo. But he has you now. He needs you."

Something in Luca's gaze shifts, a raw vulnerability peeking through before it's quickly shuttered. "I don't know how to do this. How to be what he needs. I'm not exactly fatherhood material."

I boldly reach out, laying my hand on his muscular forearm. His skin is warm, the dusting of hair tickling my palm. "You'll figure it out. You'll learn. And I'll be here, every step of the way. For Matteo."

His eyes drop to where my hand rests on his arm, then drags back up to my face. The air feels thick, crackling with a tension I can't name. Luca's gaze burns into me, searing me from the inside out. I know I should drop my hand, step back, put some distance between us. But I can't seem to make my body obey.

Finally, Luca clears his throat and steps back. He's all formality as he states with a nod, "Good-night, Ms. Johnson."

He turns and leaves before I can bid him good night as well.

Leaving me there with cheeks and body burning.

Luca Romano is a dangerous man.

In more ways than one.